TALL IN THE SADDLE

Canadian Cataloguing in Publication Data
Carter, Anne, 1953-
Tall in the saddle

ISBN 1-55143-154-8

1. Cowboys—Juvenile fiction. I. McPhail, David, 1940 -
II. Title.
PS8555.A7725T34 1999   jC813'.54 C99-910301-6
PZ7.C2427Ta 1999

Library of Congress Catalog Card Number: 99-61433

Orca Book Publishers gratefully acknowledges the support
of our publishing programs provided by the following
agencies: the Department of Canadian Heritage,
The Canada Council for the Arts, and the British
Columbia Arts Council.
Canada

Design by Christine Toller
Printed and bound in Hong Kong

IN CANADA:
Orca Book Publishers
PO Box 5626, Station B
Victoria, BC Canada
V8R 6S4

IN THE UNITED STATES:
Orca Book Publishers
PO Box 468
Custer, WA USA
98240-0468

01 00 99   5 4 3 2 1

To Craig, who rides tall in the saddle.
A.C.

To Jak and Sam
D.M.

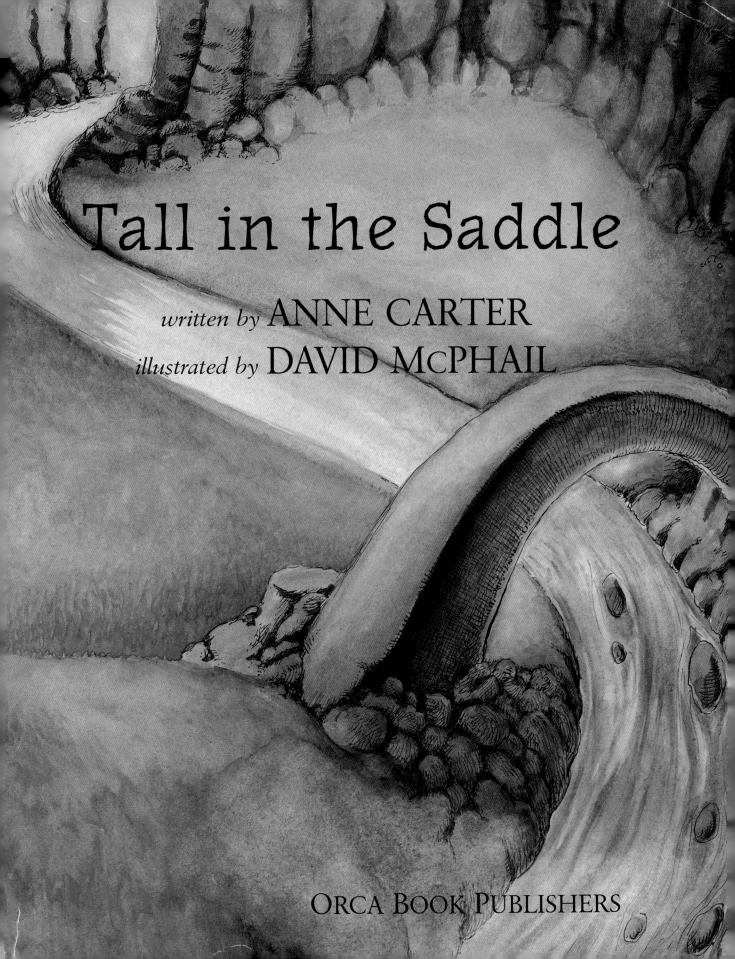

Tall in the Saddle

written by ANNE CARTER

illustrated by DAVID McPHAIL

ORCA BOOK PUBLISHERS

We play cowboys, early in the morning. Dad leaves for work in his suit and tie, still wearing his boots.

I follow him. He walks to the bottom of our street ...

slips off his jacket, tucks in his pants
and borrows Mrs. Fusspot's bike.
She left it out overnight,
forgetting about us cowboys.
With one foot in the stirrup ...

he swings up to ride a wild horse, a bronco,
front legs bucking high. "Steady, boy, steady," my dad says.
Only my dad and I can tame such a horse.

But tattletale Jen and mean-mouth Ben are watching,
running to tell. They always do.
Dad whirls his tie ... a long lasso
looping through the air ...

catching them! They're hogtied now,
four feet complaining to the wind.
Two wraps and a half hitch.
"Yeehaw," Dad hollers. The horse rears, ready to fly.

My dad rides, tall in the saddle.
One hand reaches for a piece of the sky.

The city street is now a dusty trail,

a long road of hungry cows,
mooing.
This is a job for a cowboy ...

to lead the herd to green grass and find a water hole.
Dad ties a red bandana to keep the dust off his face.
"Git along little doggie," he yells at a stray calf because ...

down in the canyon, he sees the Rotten Rustler Gang,
hiding in the shadows,
waiting for the strays.

"Giddyup," Dad cries, kicking up his heels.
He gallops,
and chases those thieves ...

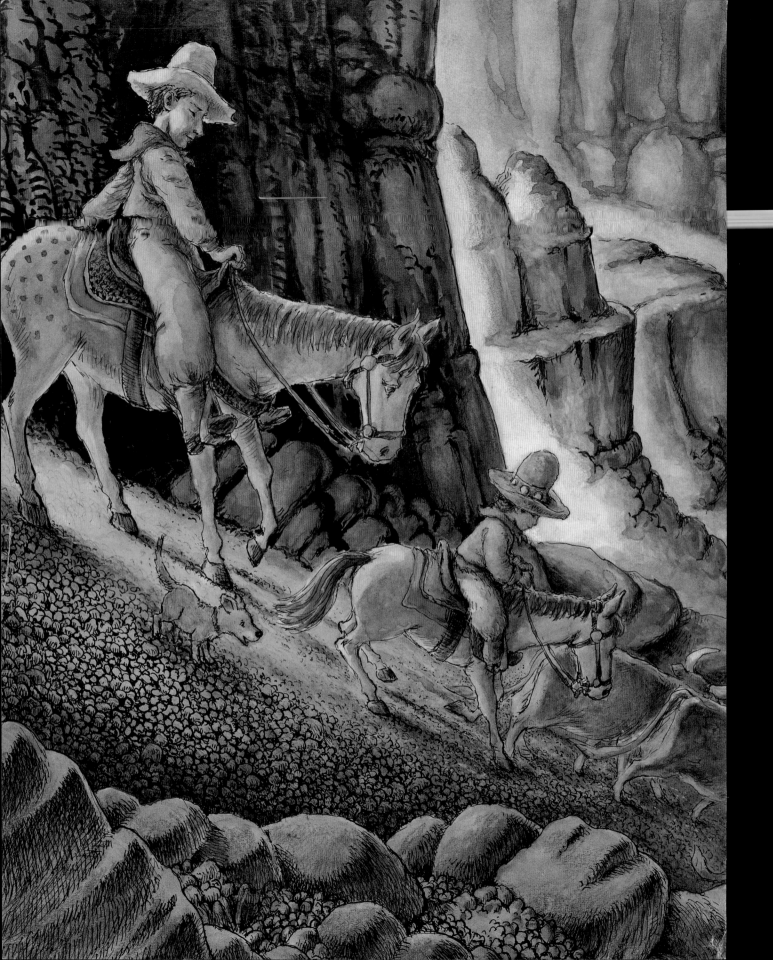

away. The herd passes through,
parks in the long grass, safe.
"All in a day's work," Dad sighs, and ...

rides back slowly, up through the city,
an orange sun behind him.
At the bottom of our street
he hears ...

tattletale Jen and mean-mouth Ben, still complaining.
With one quick tug
he sets them free.

He pats his horse good-night. It runs into the orange light.
And there's Mrs. Fusspot's bike, back again.
My dad turns to see ...

me, running to meet him.
He swings me high on his shoulders.
I ride home, tall in the saddle.
One hand reaches for a piece of the sky.